W9-AFE-700
Ackley, Iowa 50601

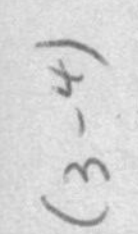

Tightly wound . . .

Park's voice sounded hoarse. "Morton? Sorry I tore your shirt."

He clutched the coarse strip of cloth between his fingers, waiting for Morton to answer, willing her to speak.

At that moment an image flashed before his eyes: the image of a mummy. A big, dead mummy wrapped in strips of coarse cloth.

A breath of air touched his face. It had a rank, ancient odor—a faintly sweet, faintly rotted smell.

Park gagged. Then he opened his mouth and shouted, "Morton!" as loudly as he could.

"Morton's gone," said a low voice. Something grabbed him by the shoulders and spun him violently around.

He was being wound up—wound up like a mummy.

"No! Let me go!" he shouted. "Hellllp. Help m—"

A strip of cloth covered his mouth.

Something spoke, close to his ear.

"Looks like you're all tied up," the voice said.

Other Skylark Books you won't want to miss!

Pronounce It Dead *by Ivy Ruckman*

The Ghost Wore Gray *by Bruce Coville*

The Ghost in the Big Brass Bed *by Bruce Coville*

The Ghost in the Third Row *by Bruce Coville*

Elvis Is Back, and He's in the Sixth Grade!
by Stephen Mooser

They're Torturing Teachers in Room 104
by Jerry Piasecki

What Is the Teacher's Toupee Doing
in the Fish Tank? *by Jerry Piasecki*

Teacher Vic Is a Vampire . . . Retired *by Jerry Piasecki*

Ackley Public Library
401 State Street
Ackley, Iowa 50601

GRAVEYARD SCHOOL

Don't Tell Mummy

Tom B. Stone

A SKYLARK BOOK
New York Toronto London Sydney Auckland

RL 3.6, 008–012

DON'T TELL MUMMY

A Skylark Book / January 1997

Skylark Books is a registered trademark of Bantam Books,
a division of Bantam Doubleday Dell Publishing Group, Inc.
Registered in U.S. Patent and Trademark Office and elsewhere.
Graveyard School is a trademark of
Bantam Doubleday Dell Publishing Group, Inc.

All rights reserved.
Copyright © 1997 by Tom B. Stone
Cover art copyright © 1997 by Mark Nagata
No part of this book may be reproduced or transmitted
in any form or by any means, electronic or mechanical,
including photocopying, recording, or by any information
storage and retrieval system, without permission in
writing from the publisher.
For information address:
Bantam Doubleday Dell Books for Young Readers

If you purchased this book without a cover, you should be aware that this book is stolen property. It was reported as "unsold and destroyed" to the publisher, and neither the author nor the publisher has received any payment for this "stripped book."

ISBN 0-553-48504-0

Published simultaneously in the United States and Canada

Bantam Books are published by Bantam Books, a division of Bantam Doubleday Dell Publishing Group, Inc. Its trademark, consisting of the words "Bantam Books" and the portrayal of a rooster, is Registered in U.S. Patent and Trademark Office and in other countries. Marca Registrada. Bantam Books, 1540 Broadway, New York, New York 10036.

PRINTED IN THE UNITED STATES OF AMERICA

OPM 0 9 8 7 6 5 4 3 2 1

GRAVEYARD SCHOOL

16

Don't Tell Mummy

CHAPTER 1

Skip Wolfson was hovering by the door of the battered yellow school bus in front of Grove Hill Elementary School when Parker Addams came charging up.

"Move," said Park. "Or you'll miss the bus."

"You're late," said Skip, never taking his gaze off the bus.

"My locker attacked me," said Park.

Skip whirled around. His eyes widened. His olive skin paled suddenly, turning greenish gray. "It . . . you . . . what . . ."

"Not *really,*" said Park. "C'mon, Skip. Get real. I just meant when I opened the door, all my books fell out. I thought for a minute the bus would leave without me."

Still pale, Skip turned back to face the bus. "Worse things have happened."

"Are you having *another* bad bus day, Wolfson? Get over it. 'Cause if you don't, you're gonna be the only kid in sixth grade who doesn't go on the class trip. And you know what that means."

Skip didn't answer. Park wasn't surprised. Ever since Skip's family had moved to the country and Skip had started riding the bus to school, he'd been psycho about buses.

"You know what that means?" Park repeated. Then he answered for Skip. "It means a day spent with Dr. Morthouse. You tell me that a ride on *any* bus is worse than that."

Park wasn't about to let Skip blow their escape. Adult authority figures were conferring nearby. At any minute one of them would notice that Skip and Park weren't on the bus and decide to do something.

"Skip," Park hissed. "You've got to get over this unnatural fear of buses." He shoved Skip. Hard. "Move!"

"Hey!" Skip turned and pushed Park back.

A familiar, sickeningly cheerful voice said, "Boys, boys! Is there a problem here?"

Park's heart sank. An authority figure had noticed them. Park shifted from pushing Skip to putting his hand on Skip's shoulder. He faced Hannibal Lucre, the assistant principal of Graveyard School, and smiled.

Skip mumbled, "No, no problem, Mr. Lucre," and bolted out from under Park's hand and up the steps to safety, his fear of buses forgotten.

Mr. Lucre rubbed his plump, pawlike hands together. As usual, he was dressed in a brown suit with a bow tie, his sparse brown hair combed across the bald spot crowning his head. "*Is* there a problem?" he repeated. His bow tie twitched against his Adam's apple when he talked. The sun glinted off his bald spot with painful, oily brightness.

Park winced. The unnatural brilliance of Mr. Lucre's pate reminded him of the steely glint that always accompanied the smile of the school principal, Dr. Morthouse. More than a few students at the school believed that glint was the glint of a hidden fang.

At the thought of Dr. Morthouse and her fang, Park glanced around nervously in spite of himself to see if she was anywhere in sight. But of course she wasn't. The principal rarely did class trips. She left that to Mr. Lucre and the teachers.

"No, sir, no problem, Mr. Lucre, sir," Park answered at last.

"You weren't fighting?" Mr. Lucre asked. He sounded disappointed.

"Fighting? Me and Skip? No! We're friends. We were just, you know, goofing. You know how that is."

Mr. Lucre looked puzzled. It occurred to Park that Mr. Lucre was not the sort of person who would understand about friends. Or about goofing.

Park eased backward and slid his foot up onto the lower step of the bus. What if Mr. Lucre decided Park couldn't go on the trip? What if he sent Park to the office—to spend the day with Dr. Morthouse?

As if he had read Park's thoughts, Mr. Lucre said, "Well . . . fighting is certainly no way to begin our little outing, is it? And I know you wouldn't want to have to stay behind with Dr. Morthouse, would you?"

"No!" Park saw himself in Dr. Morthouse's office, a student body of one—a real live *dead* student body, after a day spent with the principal.

Something in Park's voice, probably terror, brought a smile to Mr. Lucre's lips.

Park took advantage of the moment to obey the first rule of survival at Graveyard School: Run for your life.

He leaped onto the bus and tore down the aisle, trying to put as much room as possible between himself and Mr. Lucre. Looking over his shoulder, he saw Mr. Lucre's brown suit fill the bus doorway and block out the light.

Evasive maneuver, thought Park.

He flung himself into an empty seat and slid down.

"Watch it!" a gravelly voice complained.

"Watch it yourself," Park retorted automatically. He

slumped down, then leaned over to see what was happening.

Mr. Lucre had stopped to say something to a teacher sitting at the front of the bus.

A hand shot out and grabbed a fistful of Park's jacket. He felt himself raised off the seat. He turned his head and found himself eyeball to eyeball with his seatmate.

"Adapt," she growled. "Or become extinct." Her English had a faint, unidentifiable accent.

Park's eyes widened. Not only was his seatmate a girl he didn't recognize, but she was also wearing the shortest hair he'd ever seen on anyone who wasn't bald or on MTV.

"Who are *you*?" Park demanded.

The girl let him go, and he bounced down onto his seat.

"Morton," said the girl. "Who're you?"

"Morton?" asked Park.

"You're Morton too?" said the girl.

"No! My name's not Morton."

"Oh. Too bad."

"It's Park."

"Park? Your name is *Park*? Like, let's pack a picnic and go to the park? Interesting," she said. The way she said it, Park knew she meant *weird*.

"It's really Parker, and it's my father's name," said Park. "And who ever heard of a girl called Morton?"

"You just did," she said. She laughed suddenly. Her laugh was as gravelly as her voice.

The bus door closed. Mr. Lucre held up his hand. "Boys and girls," he said. "Fellow academicians." He beamed at the teachers bunched into a defensive formation at the front of the bus. "Before we begin our annual sixth-grade class trip to the museum, I'd like to go over a few rules of conduct with you. Please fasten your seat belts. Stay in your seats. No running in the aisle. No running in the museum. . . ."

As Mr. Lucre droned on, Park realized he was safe from the assistant principal, at least for the moment. He relaxed into his seat, with a sigh of relief. First his locker, then Skip doing his waltz with the weird, then Mr. Lucre pursuing Park. This day had not gotten off to a good start.

Morton was watching Mr. Lucre. Park watched Morton. She was pretty short to be so strong. She was wearing faded, baggy overalls and scuffed, intricately tooled cowboy boots. The blue sweater she wore under the overalls was almost as faded as the overalls. Old-fashioned wire-rimmed glasses magnified her eyes, which were so dark brown that they looked almost black. In contrast to the rest of her outfit, she had on heavy, elaborate dangling earrings that glittered hypnotically with every movement of her head.

Park's older sister would have killed to be allowed to

wear earrings like that to school. *Or anywhere,* thought Park.

"What a strange person," said Morton, her attention still focused on Mr. Lucre.

"Mr. Lucre? He's pretty normal—for Graveyard School."

She looked at him quickly. "Graveyard School? I thought it was Grove Hill School."

"Grove Hill is the official name," Park said. "But everyone calls it Graveyard School."

"Why?"

"You know. Because of all the sick stuff that happens here." He thought back over his own experiences, including a cruise through the school lunchroom that could have launched a magazine called *The Gross Gourmet,* and felt his stomach clench at the memory. "Also there's a graveyard on the hill behind the school. It's abandoned." He added casually, "Probably haunted, too."

Morton raised one eyebrow. "Haunted?" she said scornfully, clearly unimpressed.

Then Park raised both his eyebrows. "Hey. Wait a minute. You don't know all this?"

"Not exactly."

"Are you new? No one said anything about any new kids in class." Grove Hill was a small town. New kids were noticed.

"I've been around awhile," she said, looking uncomfortable.

"Not in my class," Park said positively. He paused. He thought. *Not new. Not in sixth grade. And sort of clueless.* There was only one solution. "You're from another class, aren't you?"

"Well . . . yes," she said.

"I knew it!" Park crowed. "I knew it. You're a fifth-grader, aren't you? That's why you're so . . ." He was going to say, *short,* then realized she might be sensitive about her height. Some people were funny that way. "That's why I didn't know you," he finished triumphantly.

Before she could answer, he went on, "But how did you get out of class to go on the sixth-grade class trip? Why couldn't you just wait your turn until next year, like all the other little kids?" Indignation overcame his satisfaction at having solved the mystery of Morton.

"I'm not a little kid!"

"You are if you're not in sixth grade," said Park smugly.

"I bet I'm as old as you are. Older!"

"You mean you got held back a year?"

"Held back a year?" she said. "What is that supposed to mean?"

"Nothing," said Park.

Morton glared at him. Then she said, "My parents wanted me to go on the museum trip. That's all."

"Whoa! Your parents fixed it up? Got you out of class so you could go to the museum?" Park fell back in his seat. Some kids had all the luck. He'd like to see the day *his* parents got him out of class.

The bus jerked forward with a gassy belch and lurched out of the school parking lot.

Mr. Lucre, who was still standing, facing the back of the bus, was thrown stomach first into his seat. A small cheer broke out among the students. Red-faced, a strand of shiny brown hair flopping over his eyes, Mr. Lucre fishtailed around in his seat and fastened his seat belt.

Park watched the assistant principal for a disgusted moment. His indignation toward Morton softened. At least *he* was a sixth-grader. When this year ended, he was finished with Graveyard School forever. As a fifth-grader, Morton had another year at Graveyard School.

Park watched with a sense of relief as the old school building receded. The Museum of Archives and Natural History might be filled with old junk, but so what? He would be far, far away from Graveyard School.

The day had gotten off to a bad start, but that didn't mean anything, Park told himself. After all, even a bad day at the museum was better than a good day at Graveyard School.

Once again, Park was wrong. Horribly, gruesomely wrong.

CHAPTER 2

"Remember, we will be using the buddy system," Mr. Lucre intoned, rising to his feet. This time, he held on to the back of his seat and lurched only slightly as the bus pulled into a parking place in the museum lot. "Your seatmate is your buddy. We will be touring various areas of the museum."

"Seatmate!" Park yelped. He looked over at Morton. "Wait a minute!"

He must have spoken more loudly than he intended, because Mr. Lucre looked his way. "Are we having *another* problem, Parker?"

"No! No," Park answered quickly. He waited until

Mr. Lucre returned to speech mode, then dropped his head to his hands and groaned loudly. Great. He had a fifth-grader for his buddy for the entire trip.

Skip walked by with his partner, David Pike, and punched Park on the arm. "Tough luck," he said.

"Why don't you take a long ride on a bad bus," Park snarled.

The smile left Skip's lips. "Not funny," he said. "Why don't you go dance with a dead mummy?"

Skip marched away. Park glared after him. "It would be hard to dance with a live mummy," he called after Skip. "'Cause they're all dead, in case you didn't know."

"Are we going into the museum or are you afraid to leave the bus?" Morton's gravelly voice interrupted his thoughts.

"Chill," said Park. *A bad day at the museum is better than a good day at Graveyard School,* he reminded himself as he stomped down the aisle and off the bus.

"Park, you and uh . . ." Mr. Lucre hesitated. Then he waved his hand. ". . . your buddy are in Ms. Camp's group."

That cheered Park slightly. He liked Ms. Camp. As teachers at Graveyard School went, she was actually close to normal, even if she sometimes was kind of disorganized.

Ms. Camp led the group into the museum, her lips

moving as she read over a list she held. At the information desk she stopped and turned. She studied the list, frowned, and then groped in her waist pack for a pen, apparently forgetting about the pencil she had stuck behind one ear. She adjusted her glasses, and the pencil fell to the floor. She bent to reach for the pencil and her glasses slid off her nose and fell too.

Polly Hannah, perennial teacher's pet, leaped forward and picked up the glasses and the pencil to hand to Ms. Camp.

"Thank you, Polly," said Ms. Camp. She stared blindly at the two objects for a moment. To Park's relief, she put the glasses on her nose and stuck the pencil behind her ear. She made a note on her list with the pen and stuck it behind the other ear.

"Of course, Ms. Camp. It's only what any good student would do," said Polly. She ran her fingers through her yellow curls and adjusted her *faux* rabbit fur headband.

"Gag me," muttered Park.

Ms. Camp smiled distractedly, then cleared her throat. "We're going to visit a number of exhibits, including, of course, the new Egyptian section, on loan from the National Museum of Archaeology," she said. "We—"

"Are we going to visit the precious stones?" Polly cried shrilly. "That's my favorite." She smirked. "My mother says you can never have too many diamonds.

I'm going to get diamond earrings for my sixteenth birthday." Polly had just gotten her ears pi[illegible] she'd been a show-off pain about it ever sinc[illegible] she was a show-off pain about practically [illegible]

"Diamonds are an artificially inflat[illegible] Christopher Hampton, the class finan[illegible] would be a better investment."

"I already *have* gold earrings," [illegible] insulted. "You have to get real gold [illegible] get your ears pierced or they might [illegible]

To Park's surprise, Morton sud[illegible] "You call those earrings? Those little bit[illegible] gold?"

Polly spun around, ready to trash Morton. Her eyes focused on Morton's earrings, and the words died on her lips.

Ms. Camp clapped her hands. "Okay, everybody, listen up. Stay with your buddy. If you get lost or separated, go to a museum guard and tell him or her. If you can't find a guard, come to this desk and tell the person in charge. I don't think I need to remind you of the consequences of losing your buddy."

She paused to let the veiled threat sink in. Then she patted the information desk beside her. She looked down at her notes. "And now, I'd like to introduce our guide on our museum tour, Mr., Mr. . . ."

A museum guide stepped out from behind the information desk to join them. Ms. Camp leaned forward to peer at his name tag, then said triumphantly, "Mr. Halsey!"

"Thank you," said Mr. Halsey. His voice was flat. He looked like a low-rent Arnold Schwarzenegger in his too-tight blue suit. He had a crew cut and narrow, watchful blue eyes. "Welcome to the museum. We have many adventures in store for you today."

"Yeah, right," muttered Park.

"So if you will follow me," Mr. Halsey continued, "we'll begin in the Hall of the Terrible Lizards."

"Dinosaurs!" whined Polly. "I want to see the precious gems."

"We will, Polly," said Ms. Camp.

"You silenced Polly. Totally. That was excellent," said Maria Medina, joining them in the line. "But who *are* you?"

"Morton," said Morton. "Who are you?"

"Maria," said Maria, looking surprised.

"Morton's in the fifth grade," Park explained quickly. "Her parents fixed it so she could come on the trip."

"Lucky," said Maria. She smoothed back her dark bangs, which promptly fell forward to cover her straight black eyebrows again.

"Cool haircut," said Stacey Carter, who was Maria's buddy for the day, as well as her best friend. Stacey wore her brown hair in its usual single braid at the back. Although Stacey didn't wear matching outfits with coordinated stockings the way Polly often did, she didn't dress quite as casually as Maria (who had the world's largest collection of rugby shirts) or Park or most of the other kids in the class. That was because she ran a dog-walking and pet-sitting business and had work to do most days after school.

"I wish my parents would let me get my hair cut like that," said Maria.

"It's a wig," said Morton.

"A wig?" said Stacey, startled.

Morton burst out laughing.

"Oh," said Stacey.

"Fifth-grade humor," said Park. He rolled his eyes.

Maria said, "I thought it was pretty funny."

"Thank you," said Morton. She raised one eyebrow at Park with a smug expression.

Park crossed his eyes and pretended he was putting his finger up his nose.

"Sixth-grade humor?" asked Morton.

"Class, let's go," said Ms. Camp.

The museum was big. They followed halls from one end to the other, climbed stairs and boarded elevators. Their footsteps echoed off the polished granite floors. Their voices echoed off the high, vaulted ceilings.

"This is an old museum," remarked Morton. "Older than most museums around here."

"How do you know that?" asked Park.

Morton shrugged.

"Have you been to lots of museums?" asked Maria.

"With my parents," Morton answered.

"Wow," Maria said. "They must like old stuff."

Morton made a face.

Mr. Halsey held up his hand. Ms. Camp motioned for everyone to come forward. After a few minutes of confusion, they had assembled in a half circle around the guide.

"We are now entering the Hall of the Terrible Lizards," said Mr. Halsey. "These are the bones of creatures that lived millions and millions of years ago, before humans walked the earth. Had humans lived at the same time as the dinosaurs, humans might have become extinct. Ha, ha."

Next to Park, David Pike muttered, "Ha, ha, *ha*. So funny I forgot to laugh." David's little brother was a dino-head, but after a bad experience with a nasty science teacher and a science report that had gone very, very wrong, David had lost interest in dinosaurs forever. Now dinosaurs did for David what buses did for Skip.

"Some of you may be familiar with dinosaurs from the movie *Jurassic Park,*" Mr. Halsey droned on.

Morton grabbed Park's sleeve. "Hey! If you lived back then, what would your name be?"

"What?" said Park.

"Jurassic Park! Get it. Jurassic *Park.*" Morton pointed at Park.

"I get it, I get it," said Park. Both Stacey and Maria

cracked up. Park sighed and shook his head. *Fifth-grade humor,* he said to himself.

Mr. Halsey said, "Now, if you will step this way!"

"Stay together!" Ms. Camp warned.

The dinosaurs loomed up, dwarfing the kids around them. Park stared at the massive frames of skeletons, the rows of brontosaurus ribs and staircases of stegosaurus spines, the plates of armor, the spikes of bone.

"Wow," said Park, pointing overhead. "Check it out."

David looked up toward a very realistic-looking fiberglass reconstruction of a pterodactyl suspended on almost invisible wires from the ceiling, its fiberglass wings outstretched, its clawed feet trailing under it like prehistoric landing gear.

"Yuck," he said, and dodged sideways, as if he expected it to swoop down on him.

Park laughed.

"My dog, Morris, would love this place," Stacey whispered to Maria. "He loves bones."

"One of these guys could eat Morris for breakfast," Maria whispered back.

Stacey snorted. "They'd have to catch him first."

Other tourists drifted by. Their low voices echoed off the high ceilings, punctuated by the obnoxious squeals of little kids. Another tour group passed in a rattle of words and a shuffle of feet.

"I don't like this place," said David. He was turning

in slow circles, as if his life depended on keeping the whole room under constant surveillance.

Unexpectedly, a wave of sleep washed over Park. He yawned, his jaw cracking, his eyes watering.

He shuffled forward with the group, trying to concentrate on Mr. Halsey's droning voice. The guide was so dull that he could have been a teacher at Graveyard School. If the dinosaurs had been alive, they would have died of boredom.

Park yawned again. He needed something to wake him up. He took a deep breath. He shook his head, trying to clear his brain.

The class moved forward. Park drifted to the outer edge of the group. He yawned again, staring through sleep-slitted eyes at a stegosaurus model set against a painted backdrop of sky and forest. Its comparatively tiny head was lowered to a pool made with a mirror and some sand, to make it seem as if it were about to take a drink. Other dinosaurs were painted on the backdrop.

Park closed his jaws with a snap.

He opened his eyes and looked up again at the pterodactyl. He rubbed his eyes.

It's impossible, he told himself. *You're imagining things.*

But it was true.

CHAPTER 3

The pterodactyl had taken flight. It was spinning around above them in wider and wider circles, like an enormous remote-control airplane gone out of control.

One of the huge fiberglass wings grazed a wall, and a shower of plaster fell. People threw up their hands to cover their heads. Someone screamed.

Ms. Camp grabbed both her ears. Mr. Halsey's face turned an alarming shade of red as plaster powdered him, giving him a world-class case of dandruff.

At any other time Park might have laughed. But he was too busy watching the dinosaur fly.

The pterodactyl made another crazy circle around

the high corners of the room, gouging the walls, tearing out chunks of plaster and crumpling the tips of its own wings.

Park ducked. Had he seen the pterodactyl's wings move? The long beak open and close?

Before Park could be certain, one of the wires tore loose from the ceiling with a ragged groan. The dinosaur jerked against the wire that connected its other wing to the overhead support. A long crack appeared in the plaster.

"Look out!" screamed Park. "Run! Ru—"

Someone pushed him out of the way and hurried past. He saw adults grab children and charge like linebackers for the door. Shouts and wails and the pounding of feet joined the sound of crashing plaster.

Regaining his balance, Park spun toward the door—and collided with Morton.

"Get out of my way! Move!"

Morton planted her feet firmly on the floor and put her hands on her hips. She glared up at the pirouetting pterodactyl.

"This can't be happening," she said. "This isn't—"

The other wire snapped with a nasty crack. Park pushed Morton with all his might.

And the pterodactyl crashed to the floor.

CHAPTER 4

"I told you we should have gone to look at the diamonds," Polly shrieked. "Now look what happened!"

She bent over to brush plaster dust from her pink jean skirt.

"Get a life," snapped Maria. She glanced over at Stacey. "You okay?"

"Yeah," said Stacey.

Morton leaned forward to rest her hands on her knees. She was breathing heavily.

Park took a deep breath himself. Suddenly he wasn't sleepy anymore.

Without looking at Park, Morton said, "Thanks. I owe you one."

"I know," said Park. He turned his head to stare at the place where he and Morton had been standing. It was covered by the body of the pterodactyl. Its wire skeleton had ripped through and shredded the fiberglass skin. If he and Morton had not moved in time, they would have been carved into people sushi by the huge wire rib cage.

Park's knees felt funny, and his stomach felt even funnier. He'd almost been trashed by a pterodactyl—a fake pterodactyl.

But what had made it fall? He turned his attention to the ceiling. It looked as if a plane had crashed through the hole where one of the wires that had anchored the dinosaur model had been attached. The other wire, still curling and bouncing, hung from a spiderweb of cracks. If it hadn't snapped, it would have taken another chunk of ceiling with it as it tore loose.

The dinosaur lay in pieces on the ground, amid plaster and fiberglass shards and curled support wire.

Leaning forward, Park stared at the wire that had broken, and frowned. He wasn't sure, but the wire looked almost as if it had been . . . melted? He reached out a tentative finger.

"Oww!" he said. The tip of the wire had burned his

finger. The melted-looking blob of metal at the end of the wire really had melted. It was still soft.

Ms. Camp clapped her hands. "Okay, everybody, find your buddy. Let's get over here and make sure no one is hurt." Her face was pale, and her glasses were askew. She took them off to wipe off the plaster dust. Her eyes were ringed with dust, too.

A guard hurried up and caught Mr. Halsey by the arm, and the two of them conferred. The guard pointed at the group and then toward the door, and Mr. Halsey nodded.

Clearing his throat, Mr. Halsey walked back to stand next to Ms. Camp. "Is *everyone* accounted for?" he asked.

"Yes," said Ms. Camp. She put her glasses on and peered at the students. "Yesss . . ." Her lips moved as if she was counting. She finally nodded. "Yes."

"Good. The Hall of the Terrible Lizards has been closed."

"I'm shocked," muttered Park sarcastically.

"And," Mr. Halsey went on, "I think it would be best if we continued our tour somewhere else. And afterward, the museum would like to treat you all to lunch."

Polly Hannah said, "I want to talk to my lawyer. When my mother hears about this, she's going to sue!"

"Couldn't we eat now?" asked Jaws Bennett. Jaws was famous for his ability to eat anything, anytime, anyplace. He often boasted that there was nothing he wouldn't eat, not even roadkill. Park suspected it was true. Jaws had been known to eat every last bite on his tray in the Graveyard School cafeteria, then try to wheedle second helpings.

"Stay with your buddies. Stay in line," Ms. Camp said, ignoring Polly and Jaws. "Remember, there will be severe consequences if you get separated from your partner—and I don't just mean getting lost."

"Yeah. Like you get a dinosaur dropped on your head," Maria whispered loudly to no one in particular.

Ms. Camp ignored that, too. She adjusted her glasses, produced another pencil from her waist pack, stared at it for a moment, then shoved it behind her ear. "Ready, class?"

The class marched out of the museum hall. Still in slow motion, Park lagged behind until he was the last one in line. As he walked past the museum guard, he looked back over his shoulder.

The wreck of the pterodactyl lay in the center of the floor, plaster dust rising from its tattered fiberglass skin and twisted wire bones like steam from a prehistoric swamp.

"What I don't get," said Park softly as the line of kids snaked through the halls of the museum, "is how it happened. I mean, what made that bird start spinning around like that?"

"It's not really a bird, it's a dinosaur," David Pike reminded Park, slowing down to walk beside him.

"Whatever. I mean, it's not like a hurricane hit the building or anything."

"Maybe it was trying to come back to life," said David.

"It was never alive to begin with," said Park. "It's a fake. A model. Not real."

"Right," David answered. "I knew that." He paused, then added, "Still, stranger things have happened."

"You know what?" Park said. "Coming to this museum has made everybody weird. First Skip won't get on the bus. Now you think big toy dinosaurs can come to life. Get real." Park turned his back on David and pretended to be fascinated by a display case of fossil footprints under a sign that read FOLLOW THESE FOOTPRINTS TO PREHISTORIC TIMES and an arrow pointing in the direction of the Hall of the Terrible Lizards.

"Been there, done that," muttered Park.

Stacey looked back over her shoulder. "Hey, Park. You and Morton better stick with the class, or you're gonna get in trouble."

Park looked up. Stacey was standing at the foot of a long flight of stairs. The class was trudging up it ahead of her.

"Come *on*!" she said, and spun around to dash up the steps after the others.

Deciding he'd had enough trouble for one day, Park hurried toward the stairs. Then he stopped. Where was Morton?

He turned. There she was, all the way at the other end of the hall, talking to a guard.

"Morton!" he called, and waved.

She said something and gestured. The guard shook his head and pointed. She nodded.

"Morton!"

An older couple turned to give him a disapproving stare. A thickset young man holding a stack of folders glanced over at Park and said, "Shhh!"

Morton said something else to the guard and smiled. Then she glanced up and down the hall as if she couldn't make up her mind which way to go.

"Mor-tonnn!" he repeated, trying not to shout.

The older couple moved away, their shoulders stiff with disapproval.

At last Morton looked in his direction. He waved both arms. She started toward him, walking slowly. As she got closer he said, "Will you come *on*? Why are you trying to get me in trouble?"

"What are you talking about?" she asked.

He sighed. Then he said with exaggerated patience, "If you'd been here where you were supposed to be, you would have heard Ms. Camp remind us that any kids getting separated from their partners are gonna get killed."

"I'm terrified," said Morton, rolling her eyes.

"You will be, if Ms. Camp turns you over to Dr. Morthouse."

Morton gave him a bored look. "This is a dumb tour," she said. "That guide, Mr. Halsey? He could make an earthquake dull."

The class had long since disappeared from sight—and from hearing. Park grabbed Morton's shirt sleeve. "Come on!"

Her thin, tan fingers closed over his in a sudden, surprisingly powerful grip. "Don't grab me like that," she said, her dark eyes flashing.

"Then quit goofing and let's go," Park said.

She looked down the hall one more time and frowned. Then, to Park's relief, she began to climb the stairs.

To his even greater relief, they caught up with the group just as it was filing past Ms. Camp into the Cave of Diamonds, which was the museum's name for the exhibit of precious gems and minerals. Ms. Camp didn't seem to notice that they had rushed breathlessly up to join the group at the last minute. She was busy checking names off her list.

"Park," she murmured, hardly glancing up. "And, er . . ." *Check, check* went her pencil.

Park stopped short just inside the entrance. A huge rock, split in half, revealed a hollow center filled with purple crystals. "Nice geode," he said.

Ms. Camp drifted by, zipping her pack shut. "Time to listen to our guide," she said. Reluctantly Park followed her, giving Morton a sharp warning look to make certain she did too.

"Cool," said David. "A meteorite."

"A piece of one, actually," Mr. Halsey corrected him. "It fell to earth in a farmer's field not far from here in 1957. It is composed of . . ."

"Puh-lease," muttered Morton.

Even though Morton had a lot of attitude for a fifth-grader, Park had to agree with her. He wondered if Mr. Halsey was a failed schoolteacher—someone who was so dull that not even the teachers' union would let him in.

He pondered that possibility as Mr. Halsey led them past the mineral formations on display, then past a mural showing the layers of the earth's surface.

"When are we going to get to the jewelry?" Polly complained.

"Jewels are just rocks," said Mr. Halsey.

"Great," cracked Skip. "How much money do you want for that big rock over there?" He pointed.

"Oooh," said Polly. She darted away from the group and practically flung herself against the thick glass protecting the huge, blue-white diamond that sparkled behind it.

Mr. Halsey smiled thinly. "The Farthingale Diamond," he said.

"Now *that's* a rock," said Morton, deserting Park to join Polly.

"Wow! Come look at this big red ruby!" exclaimed Maria.

"Actually, that's the Gordon Garnet, excavated from the Gordon Mountain Mines during the gold rush of . . ."

But the class had ceased paying attention. The students spread out in front of the cases of gems that glittered and glistened in pools of light on velvet backgrounds.

More to keep an eye on Morton than because he was interested in diamonds and rubies, Park drifted over to join her. Polly had moved on to a necklace of pearls and gold that had supposedly belonged to Bloody Mary, the English queen who had had the unfortunate habit of killing her subjects when they wouldn't conform to her religion.

Polly probably would have been Bloody Mary's best friend, thought Park wryly. He peered down at the enormous Farthingdale Diamond. It glittered as white as an eyeball, flinging off flecks of light like sparkling tears. In the cases set into the wall on either side of the diamond, the other stones seemed plain and dim. Park barely noticed them.

Morton stepped back. Her hand went up to touch one of her ornate earrings. Her eyes stared unblinkingly ahead. Park followed the direction of her gaze.

"Hey," he began.

"Haunted, you know," said a voice behind them.

"Huh?" Park said.

But the owner of the voice wasn't talking to him. She seemed to be talking to her notepad, upon which she was sketching with rapid motions.

"Why don't you just take a picture?" Park asked.

"No photographs without permission of the museum curator," said the woman without looking up.

"Haunted? What do you mean, haunted? The diamond is haunted?" asked Morton.

"Oh, no," said the woman, looking up at last, her eyes glittering as brightly as the diamond. Park noticed that she was dressed in the same color as the velvet in the diamond case, deep midnight blue. A midnight-blue cape hung from her shoulders almost to her ankles. Even for tourist fashion, Park thought, it was a little extreme.

"Let me guess," said Park. "The museum is haunted, right? That's why we were almost killed when that pterodactyl model went ground zero." He was kidding—sort of.

The woman's impossibly bright eyes grew even brighter. "You were almost killed?"

"Morton and I were standing right underneath it. We would have been the first humans in the history of the world ever killed by a dinosaur."

"Ah. Interesting."

Morton said, "It wasn't a real dinosaur, Park. And it was just a freak accident."

"Freaked *me* out," said Park, borrowing a phrase he had heard his father use.

But Morton was ignoring him. She had turned back to survey the display cases. The artist snapped her notebook shut and turned. Her shadow fell across the diamond for a moment, and to Park, it looked as if the diamond winked. A cold, vicious chill gripped his spine.

"Ah, Morton?" he said.

The artist paused. She looked over her shoulder at Park and Morton. Her gaze was unblinking, unnerving. But Park couldn't make himself look away.

"All jewels of any real worth are haunted," said the woman softly. "Some are haunted only by human greed. Others are set in a greater human darkness."

Swallowing hard, Park managed to say, "What are you, some kind of fortune-teller?" But his voice didn't sound convincing, even to his own ears.

The artist shifted her gaze from Park to Morton. "Hauntings," she said. "How humans fear them! But there are things worse than ghosts, now—aren't there?"

Then she was gone.

CHAPTER 5

"Who was that?" asked Maria.

"Some Froot Loop," said Park. "An artist."

Morton had turned once again to the display of jewels. But she was no longer staring at the diamond. Her gaze wandered up and down the velvet-lined cases behind the thick glass, each holding a display of precious stones under tiny spotlights.

"Morton. Hey, Morton! Snap out of it!" Park almost punched her on the arm, then remembered how bent she'd gotten when he'd grabbed her sleeve and thought better of it. He waved his hand in front of her face.

She blinked. "W-What?"

"You know why you're not supposed to talk to strangers? Because they're strange, that's why. That woman just proved it."

Morton seemed to replay Park's words in her head. Finally she smiled. "Oh. Yeah. Right," she said. "What a weirdo."

"Saying stuff about ghosts and haunted jewels and saying there was even worse stuff around . . . ," said Park.

He expected Maria to laugh, even if Morton didn't. In spite of several encounters of the inhuman kind that Maria, as well as others at Graveyard School, had experienced, Maria always insisted that she didn't believe in ghosts.

But Maria didn't laugh. "Haunted," she said softly. "Well, if I was a ghost, I'd hang out in a museum."

"Why?" asked Morton.

"Because it's full of hundreds of old, dead things," said Maria. "Lots and lots of company."

As they walked out the door of the gem room, Park found himself once again lagging behind, checking over his shoulder. No pterodactyls came swooping toward him out of the shadows near the ceiling. The tourists passed back and forth in front of the cases of gems, staring at the jewels that lay inside like exotic fish in an aquarium. It was a popular exhibit, and the room was crowded.

But the woman in the cape was nowhere in sight.

Impulsively, Park stopped in front of the guard who stood at the entrance to the gem exhibit. Park smiled, trying to look like a friendly, innocent kid.

"Hi!" he said brightly.

The guard lowered her chin and surveyed Park. She smiled, the same sort of official, thin-lipped smile used by Mr. Halsey, the guide. Park wondered if they learned their smile techniques at some special museum school of smiles.

"Hello," she said. "Are you lost?" She looked pointedly in the direction in which Park's class was heading.

"Not yet," said Park. "I was just curious. This museum—it's not haunted or anything like that, is it?"

The guard's eyes widened. The tight smile vanished. She drew her thin lips together until they almost disappeared. "Haunted?" she said.

"Yeah. You know, boo, ghosts, ectoplasm. Like that."

"That rumor is completely unfounded," said the guard.

"Rumor?" asked Morton unexpectedly. "So some people *do* think this place is haunted. Has this been going on long?"

"No!" said the guard. "I mean, no, it's not haunted."

"Give me a hint," said Park. "Where does the ghost

hang out? Here? With the dinosaurs? Does it have a head? Does it drip blood?"

All those years at Graveyard School, stalking specters and dodging danger, from the supernatural to the merely subhuman teacher, had paid off. Park could go eyeball to eyeball with the guard, no problem.

It was the guard who blinked.

Her eyelids fluttered.

"Well?" demanded Park.

The guard glanced left, then right, before leaning forward to whisper hoarsely, "Second floor. West wing. *Stay away from it.*"

Before Park could cross-examine her, she straightened. She drew in her chin, sucked in her stomach, and did everything but salute. "Your class went that way, sir," she said in a loud, firm voice. "Enjoy your visit to our museum."

Park looked up just in time to see a museum guide leading another group of tourists past. The guide nodded at the guard. The guard nodded back, at the same time giving Park a firm push out the door.

"Okay, okay, okay. I can take a hint," Park said.

To Park's surprise, Morton fell into step with him. Park wondered if she was secretly afraid of ghosts after all. Had the possibility of being lost in a haunted museum made her decide to stop wandering off?

He glanced sideways at her. She was looking around

the museum, acting like a tourist. She wasn't acting afraid at all.

Which just proves that she's no sixth-grader, thought Park glumly. *If she was, she'd be smart enough to be scared—because something is wrong at this museum.*

And Park was pretty sure that whatever it was, it was just going to get worse.

"Where are we going *now*?" Polly asked. "My feet hurt."

"We're going to the west wing. It's not far," Ms. Camp said. "We'll take a break in just a little while."

The west wing? *From the guard's lips to Ms. Camp's ears,* Park thought. Had Ms. Camp been listening? But no—not even Ms. Camp, Graveyard School teacher though she was, would deliberately take the class on a haunted tour.

"We could take a break now," Park blurted out. Polly looked at him in surprise.

Ms. Camp glanced at her watch and shook her head. "Not just yet."

"But that's when accidents happen," Park said. "When you're tired. If we take a break, we might avoid an accident."

Now the rest of the class was looking at him in surprise too. Park felt stupid to the max. But he also felt extremely endangered.

Ms. Camp gave Park a smile that was meant to be

reassuring. "Don't worry, Park. I'm sure we won't have any more accidents."

"Most unusual," Mr. Halsey put in. "What happened in the dinosaur exhibit. Never heard of such a thing. Never. Ever."

"But—"

"Park is a chicken, Park is a chicken," whispered Skip.

Park gave Skip a dirty look. "Bus off," he snarled.

Skip recoiled.

"Come along now, class," said Ms. Camp.

"Say something," Park said to Morton. "You heard what the guard said."

"That guard was just yanking your chain, Park." Morton had stopped to study a map of the museum. Was she checking out the emergency exits? *Not a bad idea,* thought Park.

"Ms. Camp?" Morton said suddenly. "Where are we going?"

"To our doom," said Park. "Didn't you hear Ms. Camp?"

Morton made an impatient gesture. To Ms. Camp she said, "I mean, what exhibit?"

Mr. Halsey cleared his throat again. "I'm glad you asked. A good question. We are on our way to a special exhibition on loan from the National Museum of Archaeology that is traveling around the United States. As we head in that direction, I'd like to give you a little background. Most of you, I am sure, have heard of the pyramids of Egypt, of the great tombs of the Pharaohs, full of treasure . . ."

"The Egyptian exhibition. Cool," said Maria to Stacey. "I hope we get to see a real live mummy."

Stacey said, "A real dead mummy, you mean. Dead, and wrapped up in strips of cloth. Yuck. Talk about fashion victims."

But Park had stopped listening when Maria had said the word *mummy*. Mummies. He knew about mummies—tales he had read in books, movies he'd seen; mummies lumbering at large, stalking the arrogant archaeologists who'd disturbed their rest. They'd even studied it in class, how the tombs of the ancient Egyptians were guarded not only by secret passages and false entrances, but also by horrible curses that fell on the heads of whoever disturbed the burial chambers.

Park raised his hand. "Uh, Mr. Halsey?"

"Yes?"

"This exhibit—it's not one of those cursed exhibits, is it? You know, the kind where whoever messes with the tomb and all that is going to die a horrible, disgusting, slow, painful death?"

"What?" Mr. Halsey's flat voice sharpened. "Who told you that?"

"No one. Not exactly. It's just that—"

"Well, it's not true. Curses on tombs! Hah. What a lot of superstitious nonsense. Our museum's Hall of the

Pharaoh is perfectly safe. And it is *not* haunted.'' The guide wheeled around and jabbed his finger against the elevator's Up button.

"Get a grip, Park,'' said Stacey as Mr. Halsey and Ms. Camp herded them into the elevator.

"Haunted? Who said anything about it being haunted?'' asked Park. "I asked if it was cursed.'' Clearly, the guide knew something that he wasn't telling them.

Park looked over at Morton, hoping she'd back him up, tell the others what the guard had told them. But Morton was already getting into the elevator, her face blank, as if she'd never seen Park before in her life. Great. Now even fifth-graders were embarrassed to be seen with him.

"Come *on*, Parker,'' said Ms. Camp.

Feeling as if he was making a very, very bad mistake, Park got into the elevator and followed his class to the Hall of the Pharaoh.

He wasn't sure what he expected. He took his time getting out of the elevator, earning a sharp warning look from Ms. Camp. Looking at Park, she said to the class, "Stay with your partners, please.''

Park realized that Morton had gone to the front of the group. What a pain she was!

With a sigh, Park pushed his way through the others to stand by Morton. "Thanks for all your help back there,'' he said.

"I heard what the guard said," Morton answered. "But it doesn't mean I believed her."

"You don't think it was just a little suspicious that Mr. Halsey started talking about this place being haunted, when I hadn't even asked him about that?"

"Suspicious, yes. That doesn't prove that a ghost exists, though. It only proves that people have been talking about it."

"Check it out," said Park. "A giant pterodactyl almost ends our museum visit, permanently. A museum guard says the place is haunted. Mr. Halsey denies it's haunted without our even asking."

Morton held up her fingers. "One, the first incident was an accident, that's all. Two, the guard was repeating gossip. Three, Mr. Halsey had obviously heard the gossip and was trying to head it off. Four, you are getting on my last nerve."

They walked into the Hall of the Pharaoh. They had to wait at the entrance, a narrow doorway set into a huge wall of cut block. Limited access, Mr. Halsey explained, for security and because the exhibit itself had been set up to mimic the actual tomb where this pharaoh had been buried. "I'm sure you've read about this remarkable discovery," he said. "Of course, you probably know this pharaoh, or king, by the popular name the press has given him—King Pet. If you will remember, when the tomb of Tutankhamen was discovered, the press dubbed him King Tut. Like King Tut, King Pet was also a lesser king, which may account for the fact the tomb remained undisturbed by grave robbers . . ."

"King Pet? Sounds like cat food," remarked Stacey.

Another group came out with a guide, and Mr. Halsey led the way into the tomb of King Pet.

The walls seemed to close in on Park immediately. He knew it was all a fake, that the drawings and paintings on the cut stone were imitations, knew that the pictures of Egyptians hunting, boating on the Nile, reclining in chairs at feasts, holding ceremonies at court weren't real. But they made him uneasy.

And although the corridor was well lit, the turns and angles made shadows. The voices of his classmates grew hushed as they shuffled along, reading the descriptions of the scenes on the walls and listening to Mr. Halsey's drone.

Park stopped in front of a drawing of a boy with straight black hair and black bangs beneath an elaborate headpiece showing that he was royalty. The boy's eyes were dark and elongated with kohl. His chest was bare under an ornate gold breastplate. He had one arm drawn back, clutching a spear as he confronted a huge beast.

"Wow," said Park.

"Yeah, right," said Morton. "Like that really happened. Like the leading family back then didn't have public relations people, spin doctors, the same as politicians and movie stars do now."

That stopped Park. He'd never thought about it that way before. "You don't think this actually happened?"

"You know who gets to write the history books? The people in charge," said Morton.

Ahead of them, Polly had halted in her tracks, staring at an elaborate gold bracelet worn by a queen. "I'd die for a bracelet like that," she said.

Maria said rudely, "It can be arranged. Will you move?"

Giving Maria a nasty look, Polly walked down the passageway and around a corner.

The tunnel slanted downward, then upward again. It curved left, then right. Side passages branched off, blocked by rubble and signs that said FALSE PASSAGEWAY: BEWARE.

"Taking a wrong turn in a false passage meant death in some instances," said Mr. Halsey's voice, floating back to them. "The false passages were rigged with boulders that crushed people, trick floors that gave way to bottomless pits, and other traps for the unwary. The skeletons of those who made a wrong turn have been found in the traps."

And in case that didn't work, there were always the curses, thought Park. He glanced over at Morton, trying to take his mind off the image of falling into endless darkness in a bottomless pit, falling so far down into the ground that no one could hear you, no one could save you.

Except maybe the rats.

The rats. Did rats live in these tombs?

Park realized that he was staring at Morton's earrings as they swung back and forth, back and forth. The effect was hypnotic. Mesmerizing. His eyelids were getting heavy . . .

No. With a mighty effort, he tore his gaze away. His eyes focused on one of the panels, a painting of a young prince facing a slightly older princess aboard a boat on the Nile. The beams of a stylized sun poured down on the two figures.

Park leaned forward. Something about the picture looked very familiar. Uncomfortably familiar. He moved even closer, until his nose was inches away from the surface of the painting. A sudden warmth brushed his skin, as if the heat of the ancient sun had touched him.

Then, suddenly, the painting moved.

CHAPTER 6

"Wh—?"

Park jerked his head back as the water under the boat parted and a giant crocodile exploded into the air. Its jaws snapped as it thrashed, rocking the boat, almost swamping it.

The mouth of the princess opened in a silent scream. She staggered, then pitched out of the boat, straight into the mouth of the enormous beast. Her arms flew out as the mighty jaws clamped shut on her. It shook its head savagely, and blood spattered the boat, the river, the prince. Drops of blood and water lashed Park's face.

Then the crocodile was gone, as swiftly as it had come, pulling the princess under the surface of the water. The waves were crested with blood. The prince began to shake with silent—then abruptly loud—laughter.

"Aaaaah!" Park threw himself backward. *"No!"*

Faces turned toward him. He crashed into something soft.

"Get off me!" snarled Morton, pushing him roughly away.

"What happened? What is it?" Ms. Camp called down the narrow tunnel. She appeared at the turn, fighting her way back through the crowd of students.

Seeing Park, she stopped. "Park," she said warningly. "I hope this isn't one of your ridiculous pranks."

Park caught a glimpse of Polly's expression, smug and superior. Stacey looked disgusted and disapproving.

Morton said, "No. Park, ah, fell. He's fine. We're fine."

"The—the wall," Park stammered.

Ms. Camp didn't look as if she believed Morton. But unlike the other teachers at the school, she didn't seize on any excuse to get a kid in trouble. "All right," she said at last. "Please be more careful, okay?"

"Right," Park managed to gasp as Ms. Camp whisked back around the corner to the head of the line.

"The wall," Park said again, to Morton. He pointed. "Didn't you see it? You were standing right beside me."

He looked at the wall. The prince and princess stood

facing each other calmly as the boat drifted over the waves. The sun shined serenely down. No crocodile could be seen.

Morton examined the wall for a moment, then shook her head. "He's one ugly kid," she said. "But not enough to scream about."

"It moved," Park said. "The picture moved. A big alligator came out of the water—"

"Alligators don't live in Egypt," interrupted Morton impatiently.

"Crocodile, then. Whatever. It was huge. It jumped right out of the water and ate the girl in the boat, and the boy started to laugh."

"*Did* he?" asked Morton. She studied the picture more closely now, her eyes narrowing.

"I'm serious," Park said. "I saw it."

"Well, whatever you saw, it's not there now," said Morton. Her voice grew louder. "All I see is a picture of a really ugly *little* boy."

Park took a long, shaky breath. He stared at Morton, then at the backs of the kids vanishing along the tunnel. Mr. Halsey's voice had dwindled to a faint, persistent, sluggish drone.

"Fine," said Park at last. "Fine. Laugh at me. You'll be sorry." He didn't care if Morton was his buddy for the day. He didn't care what Ms. Camp did if they got separated. He turned and stormed back down the tunnel. Let whatever was skulking around in this tomb, in this museum, do what it wanted to the rest of his class. He was going to save himself while he still had a chance.

"Park," said Morton.

Park kept walking.

"Park, where are you going? You know we're supposed to stay together."

Park ignored her.

"Park!"

"See you around the pyramid," he snarled over his shoulder. He heard footsteps behind him. He ducked around a corner and impulsively scrambled over a pile of rocks blocking one of the fake passages. He ducked down as Morton hurried by.

"Park," she called.

Park heard her footsteps slow down. "Park?"

He peered over the pile of rocks. Morton had stopped at the far end of the passage. She put her hands on her hips. She stomped her foot.

"Okay, this isn't funny," she said. "I've had enough of your stupid idea of fun. Get out here right now or you're going to be in big trouble."

Whoa, thought Park. She sounded exactly like an authority figure. In fact, she made his sister on a particularly bad day sound sort of good. Not only was she a short fifth-grader with a buzz haircut, but she was a control freak too.

As quietly as he could, he climbed back over the rocks. He crept down the narrow corridor.

Morton stomped her foot again. "I mean it. Come out right now, you stupid brat!"

He was right behind her now. He straightened up, jumped out, and punched her shoulder. "Gotcha!" he cried.

Morton screamed, leaped straight into the air and came down swinging. Her first punch caught Park's ear.

"Owww!" He threw out his hand and blocked the second punch before it could connect with his stomach. "Hey! Don't you think you're overreacting?"

Morton drew back her arm, her hand still balled into a fist. She was panting as if she had run a long distance, and her eyes glittered in a way that made Park uneasy. "You," she gasped. "You!"

"Who did you expect? King Pet?" asked Park.

Morton looked wildly around. She swallowed hard. "That was stupid," she said. "You could have been seriously hurt."

"No kidding," said Park, rubbing his ear. Then he frowned. "Hey, why are you so psyched out? I thought you didn't believe in curses and ghosts."

"I don't!" said Morton. "Anybody would scream if someone sneaked up behind them and grabbed them."

"*That* wasn't an ordinary scream. That was the mother of all screams," Park said.

"We'd better get back to join the others before we get in trouble," Morton said.

Park folded his arms. He knew he was right. Morton

was holding out on him. Deep down, she wasn't as tough as she acted. "Not me. I'm not going anywhere but home. I don't care if I get expelled from Graveyard School. In fact," he added darkly, "they'd be doing me a favor. At least I'd live past sixth grade."

"Don't be silly," said Morton. "We should stay with the group. It's much safer."

"Safer?" asked Park. "Safer for whom?"

But before Morton could answer, the lights of the museum flickered.

Then they went out.

Park blinked. At first he didn't believe his eyes. He blinked again: darkness with his eyes closed, darkness when they were open.

The lights of the museum had definitely gone out.

From what seemed like a great distance, he heard screams and shouts.

"Morton?" he said.

"I'm right here," she said. She sounded more annoyed than frightened.

Park reached out and caught her sleeve. To his surprise, she didn't push him away.

"It's probably nothing," he said. "If we stay right here, they'll probably come back on."

"I think we should go back to join the class." Morton's voice came to him out of the inky darkness. It wasn't the dark of nighttime, with shadows and grayer areas where light from streetlights or rooms or passing

Ackley Public Library
401 State Street
Ackley, Iowa 50601

cars filtered through. It was a smothering darkness, a wall of darkness.

"Bad idea," said Park.

"We just turn around and follow the wall," said Morton reasonably. "What's so hard about that?"

"What about those fake passages?" Park said. "What if we turn down one of those?"

"They're blocked," said Morton. "C'mon, Park."

"All right, all right," Park grumbled. "You go first."

He tightened his grip on Morton's arm. He waited.

And waited.

The distant cries of his classmates grew softer, less shrill. He thought he heard, faintly, Ms. Camp's voice rapping out orders.

"What? You chicken? Go on," said Park. He tugged Morton's arm to emphasize his words.

"Morton?" said Park.

Morton didn't answer.

"Morton!" He yanked again. The sleeve of Morton's shirt tore away in a long strip.

"Oops. Sorry," said Park.

Still Morton didn't speak.

The back of Park's neck suddenly prickled with fear. He licked his lips. His voice sounded hoarse. "Morton? Sorry I tore your shirt."

He clutched the coarse strip of cloth between his fingers, waiting for Morton to answer, willing her to speak.

At that moment an image flashed before his eyes: the image of a mummy. A big, dead mummy wrapped in strips of coarse cloth.

"M-Morton?" Now his voice was a panicked whisper.

Something moved in the darkness. Something shuffled toward him. He tried to lift his feet, but they were rooted to the floor.

"Morton, this is *not* funny," Park managed to say.

A breath of air touched his face. It had a rank, ancient odor—a faintly sweet, faintly rotted smell.

Park gagged. Then he opened his mouth and shouted, "Morton!" as loudly as he could.

"Morton's gone," said a low voice. Something grabbed him by the shoulders and spun him violently around.

He was being wound up—wound up like a mummy.

"No! Let me go!" he shouted. "Hellllp. Help m—"

A strip of cloth covered his mouth.

Something spoke, close to his ear.

"Looks like you're all tied up," the voice said.

CHAPTER 7

Park tried to speak. He tried to struggle. But his arms were being wound tightly to his sides.

Desperately he kicked out. His foot connected with something hard. The grip on him loosened. Park jerked away, feeling the strips of cloth that wound him unraveling as he did.

"Owww!" said the voice. It sounded angry.

Park took off. He stumbled over the strip of cloth, and his shoulder hit a wall. He managed to stay upright, but it was hard to keep his balance in the dark without the use of his arms.

A howl filled the black air behind him.

The sound hit Park like a hand against his back. He forced his feet to go faster.

With a crash, he hit another wall. He reeled back, then forced himself to think. If he kept one shoulder against the wall, he wouldn't pinball down the tunnel.

Leaning against the wall, he started forward again.

Then he heard it. The thing was behind him. He could smell its rank breath, could hear the shuffle of its feet.

Could it see in the dark? Was that how it had found Park? Was that how it had gotten Morton?

Morton! The thought goaded Park forward. It had gotten Morton. He had to get help, had to get out of his mummy wrappings.

His shoulder hit a corner, and he lurched around it. At the same moment, he felt something grab the end of the strip of cloth that was trailing behind him.

It yanked him back against the wall. He braced his feet. His bonds tightened, squeezing his arms. For a moment he was able to hold out against the pull. But not for long. He felt his sneakers sliding along the floor. He felt himself being reeled in like a big, helpless fish.

He braced his shoulder against the wall and pushed his feet against the floor. It was no use. Whatever was behind him was much, much stronger than he was.

Then Park had an idea. If the monster in the darkness could wind him up in the strips of cloth, why couldn't he unwind himself?

He moved forward a bit, and the strip loosened. Then he spun backward, turning in dizzy circles down the tunnel.

It was working! The mummy's winding strips were coming unwound. He spun like a top, careening off walls, stumbling, gasping. The strips fell away in loops, catching at his feet. He kicked them aside and whirled like a dervish.

Just as he spun free, just as he kicked the last loop of cloth aside, he heard the roar again. Then he heard the footsteps, not shuffling this time, but lumbering, stomping.

Park fled from the sound, throwing his hands out to touch the walls and try to keep his bearings.

Where was he? Surely he should have reached his class by now. Surely someone had discovered that he and Morton were missing. Surely someone would come looking for them.

He ran on. The footsteps ran behind, closing the distance with every stomp. The floor seemed to shake. The walls trembled under his groping fingers. He skinned his knuckles, crashed into another wall, and was thrown backward.

Now the monster was almost on him. Park threw his arms out and met empty air. His knees scraped rock.

The false passageway, he thought. Even as he thought about it, he was lifting himself over the pile of rock, hurling himself down the other side.

He fell. He saw a blinding flash of light. Then everything went dark.

"Park. Hey, Park. Wake up." Park opened his eyes. For a moment he couldn't remember who the girl with the scalp-cut black hair and intense brown eyes was who was leaning over him.

"What . . . ?"

"You must have fainted," the girl said in a gravelly, clipped voice. "You don't have a bump on your head or anything."

Hearing her voice, he remembered, then sat up. "Run!" he gasped.

She grabbed his arm and pulled him to his feet. "You're not dizzy, are you? Good. You're lucky you weren't hurt, sneaking around in the dark like that. Now come *on.*"

"Why? Where are we going?" Park remembered now how Morton had disappeared when the lights went out. "Where were you?"

"Trying to find you," said Morton in a disgusted voice. "Will you hurry? If we don't catch up with the others, Ms. Camp is going to make us stand next to her the rest of the trip, like we're babies."

It was not a nice image. Park picked up his pace. "Good idea," he said, still not quite himself. "Find Ms. Camp. Tell her what happened. Warn everyone about the monster."

Morton stopped. She looked down at her hand on Park's sleeve and made a face, as if she realized she was holding on to him. But she didn't let go. "What are you talking about, Park?"

"Monster. Grabbed me." Park kept walking, pulling her along. "In the dark. Mummy monster. Tried to wrap me in strips of cloth."

"You're not making any sense. You snuck away and fell." She paused, then added thoughtfully, "Maybe you did hit your head. I wonder if the museum has a doctor on staff."

They had almost reached the others now. Rounding a corner, they stopped at the back of their group. Everyone was talking, including Mr. Halsey and Ms. Camp. No one was listening. No one seemed to have noticed that Park and Morton had been missing.

Park's wits were returning. He said to Morton, "Something grabbed me in the dark. I thought it grabbed you too."

"We just got separated, that's all. We—"

"I was holding on to it. I thought it was you. Then I realized that you weren't dressed in basic mummy. I tried to get away and that's when it started dressing me up to match." Park shuddered at the memory. "But I got away and unwound myself, and that's when I fell over into the secret passage."

"I heard you crashing down the tunnel," Morton said. "The lights came on just as you fell into the secret passage. That's when I saw you."

"You must have seen the mummy," said Park. "The strip of cloth. It was wrapped all around me. You saw that, didn't you?"

But Morton was shaking her head. "No, Park. I didn't see anyone—or anything—except you."

Park stared at her in disbelief. "You're kidding . . . aren't you?"

She shook her head again. "Why would I kid about something like that?"

Ms. Camp decided to exercise extreme measures. She adjusted her glasses, put a pen behind one ear and a pencil behind the other, took a deep breath, and shouted, "Everyone, *be quiet!*"

Since Ms. Camp didn't usually raise her voice, that got everyone's attention, even Mr. Halsey. He stopped in middrone.

"I'm sure everyone will agree that we are having a very interesting day at the museum," Ms. Camp said brightly. "But that's no excuse not to behave or not to obey the rules. Now, I'm going to call the roll to make sure everyone is here. And then we are going to continue our tour. Right, Mr. Halsey?"

Mr. Halsey leaped to attention. "Er, right, Ms.

Camp. A momentary power outage. Nothing to be worried about."

"Good." Ms. Camp took out her notebook, groped in her hair until she found a pencil, and began to call the roll.

Park kept staring at Morton. She returned his gaze. Park said, "It really happened. I was stalked by a mummy who wanted to dress me up like his twin brother."

"Do mummies have brothers?" asked Morton.

"Not funny!" Park snapped. "I could have been killed. You could have too!"

"Park, listen. You're having a bad day. In fact, this museum is having a bad day. You got lost in the dark. You fell. You had—a bad dream, sort of. Forget about it."

"No way! I'm going to tell Ms. Camp. I'm going to warn the others."

Morton shrugged. "Go ahead. But I don't think anyone is going to believe you."

"Park?" said Ms. Camp, calling the roll.

Park opened his mouth to tell his story. He thought of Ms. Camp's reaction. If Morton didn't believe him, why should Ms. Camp? And the kids in his class would laugh at him. Make fun of him. He'd get grief for the rest of his life, or at least until the end of the school year, whichever came first.

"Park? Parker Addams?"

"Here," said Park, admitting defeat. Morton looked relieved.

Ms. Camp continued, "And you and your buddy, er . . ."

"Here," said Morton.

Ms. Camp finished the roll call. The class moved forward. Park looked over his shoulder. The corridor was empty, except for the silent murals.

He felt again the coarse white cloth winding around his arms, his neck, his mouth. He saw the crocodile leap from the water and grab the girl, spraying the water—and Park himself—with blood.

But the mural hadn't moved. There had been no blood.

The winding cloth had been gone when Morton found him. She had seen no mummy lurking in the corridor.

Am I going crazy? wondered Park. *Or is everyone else?* He felt trapped. Doomed. He wondered if he would ever get out of the museum alive.

I wish I was back at Graveyard School, he thought dully, and turned to follow Morton.

The passage opened suddenly into a bigger room. "An exact replica of the door of King Pet's tomb," Mr. Halsey said proudly. Several of the people in the group gasped. Mr. Halsey nodded in satisfaction, as if he were personally responsible for the amazing sight that met their eyes.

"The burial chamber of King Pet and the royal family," he said. Park saw four huge sarcophaguses, two next to each other in the center of the floor at the back of the room, two propped across from each other on either wall. The lids of the sarcophaguses had been removed, revealing the intricately decorated mummy cases inside.

Mr. Halsey pointed at a vase. "A mummy pot," he said, "often used for keeping the mummies of small animals."

"Euww," said Stacey, backing up.

"The word *sarcophagus* actually means 'flesh-eating stone.' " Mr. Halsey laughed a practiced laugh. "An excellent name for the stone used to make the containers for the mummy cases, don't you agree?"

"Eeeuuuw," said Maria.

"Awesome," said Skip.

If Park had been speaking to Skip, he would have agreed. Display cases shimmered with gold and silver and jewels found in the chamber. Jars and bottles, chests and baskets stood behind other ropes, spilling out priceless treasures. Curling strips of papyrus, covered with hieroglyphics, were unrolled under protective glass.

Polly darted toward a chest full of shimmering jewelry, her hand outstretched. Mr. Halsey caught her arm and pulled her back. "Look, but don't touch," he warned. He pointed to a beam of light shining down from overhead, directly onto the chest. Park looked up and realized that the ceiling was dotted with lights, each one focused on an object in the room.

"A very sophisticated security system," explained Mr. Halsey. "If anything crosses that beam of light, it sets off an alarm."

Polly pulled her hand back. "There are, of course, lovely replicas of some of the jewelry available for sale in our museum shop," Mr. Halsey went on.

"Not a good value," murmured Christopher.

Mr. Halsey ignored him. "Now, as you know, this is the tomb of King Pet, as the media affectionately call him. What you may not know is that the archaeologists made a most unusual discovery when they entered King Pet's tomb. Not only did they find his mummy, but they also found the mummies of three other people. Also, most unusually, despite the vast wealth collected in the tomb, and the numerous burial scrolls, they did not find a great deal of information about the king and what we presume is his family . . ."

Park tuned out Mr. Halsey. His attention was riveted on the four sarcophaguses. Had the mummy that had attacked him come from one of those? It had to be—there were no other mummies in the museum.

But why? Had Park been a convenient victim because he'd gotten separated from the group? But why hadn't the mummy gone after Morton?

Just then Morton raised her hand. "Mr. Halsey? Mr. Halsey?" she called.

"Yes?"

"Those security lights. If the museum's lights go out, like they did a little while ago, the security lights don't work, right?"

Mr. Halsey frowned. "Possibly. But that is hardly germane to the subject at hand. Now, as I was saying . . ."

"Cool," said Maria. "So just turn out the lights, Polly, and you can fill your pockets with jewelry."

"Ha, ha, Maria. I'm not a thief." Polly stuck her nose in the air.

Park felt a chill along his spine. He edged toward the doorway, almost without realizing it. Was that when the mummy had escaped from its coffin? When the lights had gone out?

Was it still out there?

He glanced toward the sarcophaguses again.

Oh, no, he thought. *What if more than one mummy has escaped? What if they're all out there, winding people up in strips of cloth the way spiders wrap their dinners in webs?*

Then another, even more horrible thought crossed his mind.

What if the lights go out again?

Ms. Camp glanced in their direction. She looked past Park and frowned. Park turned and saw Morton creeping away. Her movements were furtive and crab-like, as if she didn't want to be seen.

What was she up to? What was going on?

"Hey," Park said. "Hey, Morton!"

The lights of the museum flickered. Then they went out again.

CHAPTER 8

"Nobody move!" bellowed Mr. Halsey.

Park ran. He didn't know what was going on. And he wasn't going to wait around to find out.

He also knew, somehow, that whatever was happening involved Morton. She was not a typical fifth-grader, not even for Graveyard School.

"Morton!" he called, moving toward the doorway where he had last seen her. He bumped into something and fell into a cascade of metal. As his hand closed around a hard, cool, bumpy object, he realized that he had crashed into one of the baskets of jewelry.

No alarms sounded. Morton had been right about the security system.

Then he realized that although it was dark, he could see. All the main lights, including the beams of the sophisticated security system, might have gone out. But just inside the burial chamber, right above the door, a red EXIT light continued to shine.

"Morton!" Park called. His voice was loud, but the screams and shouts of everyone else almost drowned it out.

Suddenly another flicker of light illuminated the tomb. Mr. Halsey raised a cigarette lighter high. "Everybody stand still!" he ordered. *"And be quiet."*

Seeing the light, the kids crowded toward Mr. Halsey like moths toward a flame.

The tiny, flickering flame barely pierced the dark red gloom of the tomb. But it helped Park see the chests and jars and display cases and dodge them as he ran for the door.

He thought he saw Morton's face as she looked back over her shoulder.

"Morton! Wait!" he shouted.

She darted through the door and vanished into the midnight darkness beyond.

Behind him he heard Ms. Camp say, "Everybody take somebody's hand, and Mr. Halsey and I will lead you out of the tomb."

Then he plunged through the dark square of doorway after Morton.

He crashed into a wall immediately. "Owww," he moaned, reeling back. He put his hands out and, using the wall as a guide, moved around a corner and was immediately swallowed in darkness.

Now I know what people mean when they say something is as dark as a tomb, thought Park. *Great.* He thought of the mummy—or mummies—cruising the dark halls, looking for victims, and his heart began to pound heavily.

"Morton," he called. "Morton, it's me! Park. Where are you?"

Morton didn't answer. But, straining his ears, he thought he heard footsteps moving away from him.

He opened his mouth to call again, then closed it. Morton wasn't going to answer, he realized, even if she could hear him. Meanwhile, if whatever else was out there heard him, it might decide to pay him a personal visit to wrap up unfinished business.

He raised his hand and realized he was still clutching the piece of jewelry he'd grabbed when he'd fallen over the display in the burial chamber. He shoved it into his pocket. He'd worry about that later. He had more important things to think about now—like finding Morton before the mummy found her.

Or him.

• • •

Following Mr. Halsey single file, the line of students moved through the tunnel. Ms. Camp brought up the rear, leaning forward to squint through her glasses as if that could help her see through the gloom. The pictures on the walls, she noticed from the corner of her eye, seemed to take on a life of their own. The flicker of the light and shadow made the figures appear to jump, turn, move, almost to be about to speak.

The museum suddenly seemed a little too cool. Mr. Halsey had explained that it was important to keep the temperature constant and fairly low to protect the exhibits. But did the museum officials have to keep the building *this* cold? Ms. Camp shivered.

Pressed back into a corner, hidden behind a giant jar that had once held grain, Park shivered for another reason.

". . . the end of the tour for today, I'm afraid," Mr. Halsey had said as he passed. Some of Park's classmates had cheered. Some had groaned about having to go back to Graveyard School early.

Park slipped out from behind the jar when Ms. Camp was a safe distance from him. He crouched, staying low, debating whether to join them, to let them lead him back to safety.

There was safety in numbers, after all. And Ms. Camp was bound to raise a fuss when she realized that Morton was missing. She'd have the whole museum out looking for Morton, darkness or no darkness.

On the other hand, Park would be in big trouble for getting separated from his partner. That was the whole point of the stupid buddy system—staying with your partner so you didn't get lost.

Somehow, Park didn't think saying "The mummy got her" was going to convince Ms. Camp that he had done his best. Somehow, once Morton was found, he had a feeling that he might spend the rest of his life in the principal's office. Or worse.

Although he couldn't think of anything worse than that.

Staying low, he crept on. He was thinking so hard that he forgot to watch where the group was going. He forgot to look for Morton.

Until he heard the muffled tread behind him.

He jerked around, expecting the worst.

He got it.

This time, by the faint and receding glow of the lighter Mr. Halsey held up, Park saw it.

The mummy. It loomed out of the shadows toward him, trailing ribbons of old, dirty cloth.

Park froze.

The mummy came closer. Closer.

Park's eyes widened. Its eyes had an eerie, unnatural glow. And it was wearing a hat—a baseball hat!

The mummy held up one strangely distorted finger to where its lips might be. "Shhh," it breathed.

"AAAah—uh!" Park opened his mouth to scream. But before he could call for help, the mummy reached out, faster than humanly possible, and clamped its other hand, trailing bandages, over Park's mouth.

Ms. Camp and the group disappeared around the corner. Park squirmed, trying to get free.

"Shhh," the mummy whispered again. Park made a face. The mummy had a bad case of grave mouth.

Park heard Ms. Camp's voice, then the sounds of his class leaving the area. A door closed with a thump, and a key turned in a lock with awful finality. The only light left was the lurid red of the EXIT sign that bathed the hall, Park, and the mummy in a bloody glow.

Panic gave Park strength he didn't know he had. He twisted wildly and managed to tear free of the mummy's grasp.

He dropped to his hands and knees, rolled sideways, and sprang to his feet to confront the monster.

To his surprise, the mummy hadn't moved. It stood there, just out of reach, its eyes glittering as it watched Park.

Park frowned. Something about the mummy looked very, very familiar. Something about the eyes . . .

"What—Who are you? What do you want?" Park said, trying to keep his voice from cracking. "What have I ever done to you?"

The eyes flickered as Park spoke. Then the mummy

laughed, and Park knew where he'd heard that sound before. It was the same laugh he'd heard the boy in the picture give, right after the crocodile had eaten the girl.

Park leaped sideways, as if he were headed for the door.

The mummy leaped sideways too.

But not for nothing had Park survived the sixth grade at Graveyard School. The moment the mummy moved, Park was already sprinting in the other direction, his hand on one wall, running as if he were running for home plate toward the safety of the darkness and the maze of the tomb.

As he ran, he couldn't resist a triumphant look over his shoulder. Clearly the ancient Egyptians had never mastered the sport of baseball. *Eat my All-Star dust,* he wanted to chortle.

The chortle died in his throat. He scanned the passage behind him wildly. No mummy was lurching toward him, framed against the EXIT light from the door.

The mummy had disappeared.

But where? Was there a secret passage? A side way? A shortcut that would lead the mummy back to meet Park face to face?

Or was it a trick? A trap?

Park couldn't think about it. He wouldn't think about it. Blindly he turned and began to run down the nightmare maze of halls.

He didn't know where he was going. He didn't know what he was going to do.

He was just running for his life.

But he hadn't taken half a dozen steps before he froze in his tracks.

Someone had stepped out into the hall ahead of him.

She raised the candle she was holding. Her earrings swung slightly, making grotesque shadows on the wall.

"Park," she said.

Park stopped. He checked over his shoulder. Nothing.

He faced Morton without going any closer.

The candlelight made her face look hollow, and much older. She didn't look like Morton, the slightly weird fifth-grader.

"Park," she said again, and stretched out her hand. "Come on. We've got to get out of here."

Without realizing what he was doing, Park shoved his hands into his pockets and took a step back.

"Where have you been?" he asked. "Why didn't you stop when I called you?"

"I didn't hear you," Morton answered. "Will you come *on*?"

"You heard me. I know you did." Park's fingers touched the piece of jewelry he'd picked up earlier. He drew it out of his pocket slowly, thinking in the back of his mind that maybe he could use it as a weapon and throw it, if worst came to worst.

Morton narrowed her eyes. They glittered strangely in the candlelight.

Park took another step back. "What's going on, Morton?"

"Why do you ask?"

He tightened his fingers around the heavy piece of metal.

"Come on, Park. We don't have time to play games."

"I'm not playing games." Suddenly Park didn't trust Morton. "I'm just trying to stay alive."

"Don't be ridiculous," Morton said sharply. "No one's going to hurt you."

"How do you know? Who are you, Morton?" He raised his hand, and the piece of jewelry caught the light and glittered in his hand.

Glittered like Morton's eyes. Like the mummy's eyes.

Glittered like the earrings she wore.

Because it was an earring he was holding. A heavy, elaborate earring, the kind worn by the ancient Egyptians in the drawings and paintings.

And almost exactly like the earrings Morton wore in her ears.

Morton was the mummy. It was Morton.

CHAPTER 9

"Noooo!" screamed Park, and jumped toward Morton with all his might.

He heard her gasp of surprise as he shoulder-charged her into the wall and ran by. The candle fell at his feet, and he kicked it hard.

It rolled away from him and went out.

He heard her getting to her feet. He ran on, keeping his arms outstretched. He took one passage to the left, another to the right, another to the left, trying to remember as he ran which way he had turned.

But it was hopeless. He was moving too fast, and he didn't have time to stop and think.

He kept running, scraping his knuckles, jamming his fingers, bruising his knees.

"Park!" he heard Morton's voice call behind him.

Like I'm gonna answer her, he thought grimly. *Here I am, come and get me.*

He tried not to make noise as he ran, tried not to pant or shout "Ouch!" when he banged his knuckles or his knees against a wall. He crashed into something and grabbed for it. It was a giant jar, maybe the same one he had hidden behind earlier. He caught it before it could fall over and shatter and give him away.

For a moment he considered hiding behind it.

But he was sure she would find him. She had a candle.

Not that she needed it. He was pretty sure she could see in the dark. He was pretty sure, now, that she could do all kinds of inhuman things, like make fake dinosaurs fly and crash to the ground, and make paintings on walls come to life and bleed and laugh.

Then he remembered the door, the big, heavy door of the tomb.

"An exact replica of the door of King Pet's tomb," Mr. Halsey had said proudly.

If he could get to the tomb and close the door behind him, he might be safe until the lights came on. He might even be able to hold out until they found him. Once they discovered he was missing, they'd come looking for him. They might even be looking for him already.

The possibility of survival gave Park new speed. He flung both arms wide and ran forward, careening from one wall to the other, hoping his pinball progress would prevent her from sneaking around him, hoping she didn't know any shortcuts through the maze that would help her beat him to the tomb.

And then he saw it: the red glow of the EXIT light through the open door of the burial chamber.

He sprinted forward and threw himself through the door. He wheeled around.

Through blurred eyes, he thought he saw the light of a candle pricking the darkness behind him.

He put his shoulder to the heavy door and pushed with all his might.

It groaned. It moved a couple of inches.

"Close," muttered Park. "Come on, you stupid door. Close!"

It groaned more loudly. It moved a few inches more.

"Close!" Park pleaded.

"Park? Park, where are you?" Morton's voice was close now.

Much too close.

He drew back and threw himself at the door so hard that both feet lifted off the ground. He wondered if his pitching arm would ever be the same.

"Park! Park, wait!"

She was just on the other side now. He slammed against the door one more time with the superhuman strength of terror, and it fell shut with a resounding thud.

It was the most beautiful sound Park had ever heard, even sweeter than a home-run ball against the wood of his favorite Louisville Slugger.

He propped his back against the door and slid down to the ground. He could hardly breathe. Sweat poured from his face. It ran down his arms, stinging his scrapes and cuts. His shoulder ached.

He felt great. He was alive.

Distantly he heard Morton say, "Park. Park, let me in. Now!"

"In your dreams," he muttered. He felt Morton pushing against the door and braced himself for a fight.

But to his surprise, she stopped after a few attempts. Then everything was silent.

Park pressed himself more firmly against the door, closed his eyes, and settled down to wait.

He didn't know how long he had been there when he realized that he might not be alone in the tomb. Behind his closed eyelids, he suddenly saw the four sarcophaguses.

Which one *had* the mummy come from? How had it gotten out? Had the others gotten out too? Or were they still inside . . . waiting for a good reason to rise and unwind?

He wanted to keep his eyes closed. But he forced himself to open them.

The red light of the EXIT sign turned light surfaces the color of fresh blood and dark surfaces and shadows the color of dried blood. Park wondered irrelevantly why EXIT lights weren't green instead of red. Didn't they teach you when you were a little kid that red meant stop and green meant go?

Not that a green light would have made the tomb look any better.

And what good was an EXIT sign to a bunch of dead people, anyway?

I'm not *dead,* Park reminded himself. *Not even close to being mummy material.*

The vast chamber was silent. Park's breathing was the loudest sound in it. Everything else was quiet.

Dead quiet.

Reluctantly Park got to his feet. He had to take a closer look at those Egyptian coffins. If he could figure out how the other mummy had gotten out, he might be able to prevent it from happening again, especially while he was sharing the tomb with the sarcophaguses.

After dragging the heaviest of the mummy cases against the door, he picked his way carefully among the displays, noticing how red the glitter of gold was, how the red glow made some colors look black and others purple. His own skin had the unhealthy glow of a radioactive sunburn, not so different from the way his stupid older sister looked after she spent a day frying on a towel in the sun.

He paused to right the overturned basket of jewelry. Then he could delay no longer. He took a deep breath. It was like a weird game of *Jeopardy!* Which coffin would he choose? What was waiting for him behind the door of, say, Coffin Number One?

I'll get the worst over first, he decided, and forced himself to walk toward the biggest sarcophagus.

The closer he got, the bigger it looked. A shudder ran through him, and he stopped. He imagined walking up to the coffin and bending over it. In his mind's eye, he saw the lid suddenly snap open, saw a hand shoot out and grab his throat, saw a creature with white skin and bloody fangs rise up and whisper "I vant to drink your blood."

No. Wait. That was a vampire. These were mummies, not vampires.

At least he hoped they weren't vampires too.

He forced himself to go up to the giant sarcophagus. It was the size of a small boat. The lid had been propped to one side. He took a deep breath and leaned over the edge of the sarcophagus.

The mummy case inside wasn't quite as large, but it was much scarier, shaped to fit a human form. A stylized face looked blankly up at him. The body of the case was covered with elaborate symbols.

King Pet, thought Park. He put a tentative hand out to touch the case. It felt cool and smooth.

It was difficult to believe a dead king was inside.

Park had a sudden vision of the coffin opening and a hand shooting out to clamp on his wrist. He quickly pulled his hand back. He pointed at the mummy case. "Stay," he ordered.

He laughed. His voice echoed hollowly in the red-stained tomb.

The echo of laughter had barely died away when he turned and saw her.

Not the queen. She lay next to the king in her own sarcophagus in her own elaborately decorated mummy case.

The chill of the tomb turned Park's legs to ice.

Why hadn't he seen her before?

She was propped up against the wall near the darkest corner of the room, facing a similar sarcophagus across from her.

In mirror image, both sarcophaguses had their lids propped open, like doors. Both mummy cases rested upright inside. Both were decorated as the king's and queen's were.

The faces were stylized, framed by heavy hair, eyes rimmed with kohl. But he recognized her just the same.

Morton.

Morton's coffin.

He'd been hanging around with a dead kid. He suddenly heard her gravelly, oddly accented English: "I've been around awhile."

Sure you have, thought Park. *Like hundreds and hundreds of years.*

But why was she picking on him? What had he done to deserve the wrath of the mummy?

Mr. Halsey's words came back to him: "The word *sarcophagus* actually means 'flesh-eating stone.' "

Forget about it, Park told himself. He checked over his shoulder to make sure the door of the tomb was still closed.

Then he walked slowly toward Morton's mummy case.

He reached out as he had at King Pet's sarcophagus and touched the cool surface.

Behind him, the display case propped against the door of the tomb went over with a crash. Before Park could even turn, hands grabbed him and lifted him up.

He saw the door of the mummy case spring open. He jabbed his elbow backward into something soft.

He heard Morton scream.

The hands gave him a furious shove. He was in the mummy case.

The lid slammed shut behind him.

CHAPTER 10

For a moment, he couldn't think.

Then he heard laughter. The mummy was laughing. The mummy thought it was funny.

Rage swept through Park. He kicked the lid of the case as hard as he could. "Let me out!" he shouted.

A muffled voice spoke softly just outside the lid. "You're it," the voice whispered.

Park punched the lid with his sore knuckles. "I'm it? *I'm* it? When I'm through with you, you're going to wish you were dead."

He heard the sound of the mummy's laughter, farther away this time.

"Come back and fight like a . . . come back! Let me out!" Park shouted desperately.

The door of the tomb opened and closed.

"Stop! Wait!"

But it was too late. The mummy was gone. Park was alone in the coffin.

He pounded the lid. He kicked it. He shouted for help. But no help came.

At last he stopped. He drew in a long, shaky breath. *So you're locked in a mummy case,* he told himself. *It isn't the first time it's happened to someone.*

They'll find me, he reassured himself. *As soon as the lights come on,* they'll find me.

He took another breath. And held it.

How much air was in the mummy case? What if it was airtight?

What if every breath he took was one breath closer to his last?

Thrusting his hands out blindly, he tried to find the edges of the lid, tried to see if he could feel a crack, a crevice, anything that might let air in.

But he found nothing. The lid fit snugly. If any air was coming in, he couldn't tell.

He had to calm down. Breathe slowly. But the more he tried to breathe slowly, the more he felt himself gasping for air.

I won't panic, he thought, and took a shallow breath.

I won't. He let the breath out again.

Was it getting harder to breathe? Was it possible for the darkness around him to be getting even darker?

He took another breath.

The door of the tomb opened. He held his breath and pressed his ear to the lid of the mummy case, straining to hear.

He heard footsteps. They went to the center of the room and stopped.

Had the mummy come back to get him?

Park decided he didn't care.

"Help!" he screamed. *"Help me! I'm in here! Helllllp!"*

The footsteps came closer.

Park stopped screaming.

The lid of the mummy case opened, and Park fell out at Morton's feet.

He threw himself against her legs. She fell back and dropped the candle she'd been holding. It landed on its side on the stone floor, but amazingly, this time it didn't go out.

Park pushed her to one side and scrambled to his feet. She grabbed one of his ankles and yanked it. He fell again.

"Park, wait!"

"Thanks, but I think I'll pass on another coffin ride," snarled Park. He jerked his ankle free and did a belly flop across the room.

She grabbed his belt and lifted him off the floor by it.

He hung there helplessly, twisting in midair. He kicked out at her.

She let him go, and he fell. "Ugh," he gasped as the wind was knocked out of his chest.

"Will you be still and listen?" Morton asked.

"Ugh, aggh, uah," Park gasped.

"I'm sorry I had to do that," said Morton. "But you didn't give me any choice."

"Huh," Park managed to say. Then he rasped, "I . . . saved your life. That dinosaur could have . . ." He stopped. He'd been going to say "That dinosaur could have killed you."

But of course, it couldn't have.

"I know," said Morton. "I appreciate it."

"You . . . have a funny way of showing it." Park's breath was coming back now. He sat up.

"I'm trying to save your life back, if you'll just listen."

"Save my life? Save *my* life? By chasing me down the halls? By wrapping me in mummy cloth? By locking me in a coffin?" Park's voice went up in disbelief.

"Shhh!" Morton glanced toward the door. Then she squatted down next to Park. "Listen," she said urgently. "Listen carefully. I've got something to tell you. It's pretty hard to believe, I know . . ."

Park folded his arms.

"I'm a mummy," Morton whispered.

It was all too much. Park couldn't help himself. He started to laugh.

"Shhh! *Be quiet,*" Morton begged. "Have some self-control!"

"You—You're not wrapped right!" Park said, trying to get a grip. "Like I hadn't guessed, even if you didn't have your picture on your coffin."

Morton glanced toward the mummy case. She ran her hand over her short hair. "That doesn't even look like me," she said. "For one thing, in my case portrait, I'm wearing a ceremonial wig."

Not fifth-grade humor, Park suddenly realized. *Bazillion-year-old mummy humor.*

A sound in the corridor outside the burial chamber jerked Morton to attention. "Shhh," she whispered.

In spite of everything, Park found himself whispering back. "Why?"

Morton didn't move. Then, swiftly, she reached over and pinched out the candle.

"What'd you do that for?"

"Shhh."

They waited for a long, long moment. Then Morton turned and leaned down to put her face next to Park's ear. She whispered so softly that Park could barely hear her.

"We have to hide," she said. "Get back in the mummy case."

"Wha—"

"Shhh!" She clamped a hand over his mouth. Then she began to pull him backward toward the coffin.

CHAPTER 11

The lid of the mummy case closed on Park once more.

Park threw himself against it. For a moment, he thought it gave way a little.

But Morton was strong. Inhumanly strong.

He heard the lid click and lock. He'd been buried alive.

Again.

"Morton! *Morton!* Let me out! I saved your life, you dumb mummy! *Let me out of here!*"

Morton didn't answer. "You're a chicken!" Park screamed. "You have a bad haircut! Polly dresses better than you do!"

But not even these insults got Morton's attention.

Park balled up his fist and hammered the lid. He was screaming and hammering so loudly that he didn't hear the footsteps outside.

He didn't even realize the lid was opening until it suddenly flew back and he fell out.

Again.

"That's it, Morton!" he shouted. "That's it. You've had it!" He jumped to his feet and stopped.

His mouth dropped open.

"You're not Morton," he said.

"Morton," said the tall, thin boy facing Park. He was wearing baggy jeans, sneakers, and a museum sweatshirt. "Is my cousin going by that name now? Where *does* she get these names?"

"Who are you?" Park managed to say.

The boy raised the candle he was holding so that the light illuminated his face. "Morton's cousin, of course," he said.

"Morton's *cousin*?"

"I don't think we look alike, either," said the boy. "Hard to believe she and I are in the same family."

As he spoke, the boy moved closer to Park. Involuntarily Park stepped back.

He wrinkled his nose.

Mummy breath.

He recognized the smell.

And the face.

It was the same boy who had been in the picture that had come to life, the boy who had laughed when the crocodile had eaten the girl.

Now the picture seemed familiar because he'd just recognized the boy.

And the girl. They'd been older, stylized versions of Morton and her cousin.

He recognized that now.

He also recognized the breath.

"It was you," Park said. "Not Morton. It was you who chased me. It was you who tried to wrap me up like a mummy. You're the one who pushed me into the coffin."

"Yes," said the boy. He smiled nastily. "Fun, wasn't it?"

"Fun? I could have smothered in that stupid mummy case."

"But you didn't," said the boy. He took a step closer. "At least, not yet."

A movement behind the boy caught Park's eye. It was Morton. She was sneaking up on them, creeping from one pool of shadow around a display to another.

"Wait!" said Park to Morton's cousin. "What happened to your wrappings? And your hat?"

"It was a look," the boy said. "I got tired of it. Can you imagine having to wear the same thing year in and year out? Fortunately, museums are furnished with all kinds of wardrobes."

"Right," said Park, recalling the old-fashioned appearance of the glasses Morton had been wearing. He wondered which exhibit she'd borrowed those from. "And what about the dinosaur? Did you make the pterodactyl fall? How?"

The boy yawned. The smell brought tears to Park's eyes. "Elementary, my dear human," the boy said. "I melted it."

"With your breath?" Park asked.

The dark, kohl-rimmed eyes narrowed. "Are you trying to be funny?"

"Me? No. Never. I really want to know."

"I melted it," the boy repeated.

"How?"

The boy shrugged. "It's something we learned. If you concentrate hard enough, you can do all kinds of things."

"Like make stegosauruses move and pterodactyls fly," said Park.

"Yes. And pictures bleed." The boy took another step closer.

"But who are you?" Park asked desperately. He tried not to look in Morton's direction. If he did, he might break down and scream at her to hurry.

What was taking her so long?

Where was she?

"If you're trying to make me look behind myself, forget it," said the boy. "That trick is as old as the pyramids. No one's going to help you. I'd know if anyone was back there. It's one of the many advantages of being a mummy—what some might call supernatural powers of perception."

The mummy took another step toward Park. Park took another step back and felt the cold stone of the edge of Morton's sarcophagus against his hand.

Morton materialized silently behind her cousin. She began to gesture.

Park tensed his muscles. "But why me?" he asked. "Why are you picking on me?"

"You helped Morton," said the mummy. "I don't like Morton."

"And I don't like *you*!" cried Morton, throwing herself with all her might against her cousin's back.

His eyes bulged in shock. His arms flew out. Park jumped to one side as Morton shoved her cousin into the mummy case. Park grabbed the lid and shoved it across the front of the case.

The mummy's hand came out and caught Park's wrist.

"No!" shouted Park.

Morton threw her weight against the lid, and it crashed against the mummy's arm.

Park heard a muffled howl, and the grip on his wrist relaxed. He jerked free.

Again Morton slammed the lid against the mummy's arm. Another howl, and the arm jerked back inside.

"Push!" shouted Morton, but Park was already pushing. The two of them slid the top of the mummy case shut.

"The lid. Sarcophagus," Morton said. She kept one hand on the case and with the other helped Park pull the heavy stone lid across the front of the sarcophagus.

The howls grew louder. "I'll get you for this, Morton," her cousin shouted. The whole sarcophagus shuddered with the fury of his struggles.

The lid slid into place.

The howls abruptly stopped.

Morton collapsed against the front of the sarcophagus. "That should hold him," she said with satisfaction.

CHAPTER 12

Park swallowed hard. He was sweating. He was shivering. He was amazed that he was still alive.

"Do you mind telling me what is going on?" he asked.

"Sorry," said Morton. She sighed. "That was my cousin."

"Duh," said Park.

"I'm King, er, Pet's daughter."

"This is not news," he told her.

She sighed again. "I know."

"How did you . . ." Park searched for the correct words. "How did you wake up?"

"I'm not sure. It happens, I guess. It started when they found us. One minute I was asleep, the next minute I was listening to people talking in a strange language. What you would call the ancient Egyptian process of mummification isn't all that well understood, you know. Not even now."

Park wasn't sweating the technical details. "But how did you get to Graveyard School?"

"We were being transported to the museum," said Morton. "I didn't know my cousin was awake. I slipped out of the truck to take a look around—and he locked me out. I'm lucky no one discovered I was missing. That would have been a mess." Her eyes narrowed angrily at the memory of what her cousin had done. "May he be swallowed by the Nile. I was trying to find my way back when I saw your school bus and heard them saying they were going on a field trip to the museum."

"Talk about luck," said Park.

She glanced toward the two largest sarcophaguses. "I just hope my parents don't find out. If they learn I've been sneaking out, I'll be in big trouble."

"Don't worry," Park said. "I won't tell Mummy. Get it?"

"That joke is older than the pyramids and the Nile combined," said Morton in disgust.

"Thanks," said Park modestly. "But what about your cousin?" The memory of his meetings with Morton's malevolent relative made Park wrinkle his nose. "I mean, talk about one rotten mummy spoiling the barrel. Even his breath is rotten. It could kill a moose."

"A moose? What's a moose?" asked Morton.

That stopped Park for a moment. He realized that although Morton had adapted pretty well, no doubt because she had spent so much time in museums, she must not have encountered a moose yet. He wondered if this museum had a moose in a display anywhere. Aloud he said, "A moose is a big animal. Sort of like a camel, only smaller."

"Oh." She smiled. "I used to call my cousin Camelbreath. His father, my uncle, was the royal embalmer. My uncle was always a little weird too, actually."

"Hanging out with dead people will do that to you," said Park. "Not that I'm saying *you're* weird," he added hastily. He went on, "Your cousin made the dinosaurs in the exhibit move, didn't he?"

"Yes. He caused that stupid pterodactyl crash too. That's his idea of fun."

"And he made the picture move. He made the crocodile eat the girl."

"A picture of him and me," Morton said. "Not funny."

"No," agreed Park. He suddenly thought of how Morton had disappeared in the dark corridor, when he had met the malevolent mummy. "But where did you go when he was after me when the lights went out? Remember, when we were standing in the tunnel? Where did you go?"

But Morton had her mind on other things. "My uncle was always conducting bizarre experiments. I wonder if waking up like this had anything to do with that. Hmmm."

Suddenly her nostrils flared. Then her eyes began to water, and she opened her mouth in an enormous yawn. "Wow, I've been up long enough. I've got to go into repose."

"Vampires can only motor around at night," Park said. "Now, about leaving me in the tunnel to go one-on-one with your cousin . . ."

"I'm *not* a vampire," said Morton. She stood up and stretched. "I don't know what the rules are yet, but blood-sucking isn't on the menu."

"Well people-wrapping is, isn't it?" said Park, standing up too. "And sarcophagus-stuffing. Yeah. And for that matter, where were you when your cousin locked me in the mummy case?"

"Listen, I helped you out, didn't I?" Morton headed for her mummy case.

She has a point, thought Park as he accompanied her. But it still didn't answer his questions.

"Are you going to, you know, rewind?" he asked, pointing to the long, narrow bands of cloth piled on the floor of her mummy case.

Morton yawned again. "Not right now," she said. She stepped inside.

"Wait," said Park. "I have more questions."

"Drop in anytime," said Morton sleepily. She smiled. Her earrings glittered. "See you around the pyramids." She closed the door of the case.

At that moment, the lights of the museum came on. The brightness blinded Park momentarily. He had to stand still until he could see. When his eyes adjusted he realized that the chamber of the tomb was a huge mess. Things had been knocked over, smashed, spilled, and scattered.

"Uh-oh," said Park. He sprinted for the door. He was halfway down the hall when he heard voices.

"This way," said an unfamiliar voice.

Instinctively Park dove behind a large funerary urn.

Two people in guard uniforms ran past, followed by two police officers and several official-looking men and women in suits.

Park heard the door of the inner chamber open. "Just as I suspected!" cried another voice. "A robbery!"

Deciding that he'd better get out of there fast, Park dodged out from behind the urn and began to run. He pushed open the door of the exhibit and ran out into the hall.

He wasn't the only one who was running. The hall seemed to be filled with people dashing back and forth, shouting into portable phones and radio receivers, calling for lost children, or just looking dazed and confused.

Weaving in and out to avoid being trampled, Park made his way unnoticed to the information desk.

Ms. Camp was there, juggling pencils and saying, "All right, everybody, stick together. We're going to go get on the bus. We'll return to the museum another day."

Mr. Halsey was intoning, "Let's stay calm. Everyone stay calm."

Park slipped into place at the back of the group as Jaws raised his hand and said, "What about our free lunch?"

Leaning over, Park said into Stacey's ear, "You'd think Jaws would have learned by now that there is no such thing as a free lunch."

"True," said Stacey. Then she said, "Hey. Where have you been?"

"Shhh! You want to get me in trouble? Did Ms. Camp miss me?"

"Are you kidding? The only thing on Ms. Camp's mind is getting on the bus and getting out of here."

Maria said, "Where's Morton?"

"Oh." Park paused. Then he said, "Her parents came to get her." He tried to look puzzled. "I guess they'd arranged with the school to meet her here."

Maria looked as if she wanted to ask more questions,

but Ms. Camp was clapping her hands and herding them toward the bus. It wasn't easy. They might have been sixth-graders, but the day's adventures had jolted them all like a first-grade Halloween sugar rush.

"Sit where you want," Mr. Lucre said, looking almost as frazzled as Ms. Camp, when the last of the teachers staggered wearily aboard the bus. "Just *sit*!"

Skip sat down by Park. "Cool trip," he offered.

"Yeah," said Park, forgetting that earlier in the day, he'd been ready to stuff Skip into the nearest mummy case. The thought of being locked in the case sent a shudder through him.

"I just wish I'd seen the guys who offed the lighting system to rob the museum," said Skip. "You think they got anything?"

Park shrugged. He suddenly realized that the lights had come back on just as Morton had closed the door of her mummy case.

Had Morton done that?

Or had her cousin Camel-breath?

What kinds of powers did mummies have?

Suddenly Park wondered if he could believe everything Morton had told him. Somehow he didn't think he could.

As the bus pulled out of the parking lot, Park took one last look at the museum.

I'll be back, he thought.

• • •

The dark corridors of the old museum were still. The night guard finished his rounds for the hour and settled in at his desk. He yawned. He tilted his head back and after a few moments began to snore softly.

In the inner chamber of the replica of the tomb of King Pet, the lid of a mummy case opened slowly. A girl peered out. When she was sure that everything was as it should be, she kicked aside the long strip of cloth tangled around her feet.

She stepped out into the room, dimly lit except for the EXIT sign and the lights that shined on the exhibits and served as security devices. Crossing the room, she was careful to avoid tripping any alarms.

The heavy stone lid of the sarcophagus seemed like a feather in her hand as she lifted it and set it to one side.

She raised her hand and knocked on the lid of the mummy case. "Knock knock," she said softly.

"Who's there?" a hollow voice asked.

She grinned. "Morton," she said.

"Morton who?" The door of the case flew open.

Morton eyed her cousin. She grinned even more broadly. "Morton says . . . you're it!" she said. She punched him on the arm and took off.

EPILOGUE

"Clear the chamber, please," the man said.

"But, sir," one of his assistants protested. "We just got in. We haven't even started to—"

"You can start tomorrow. I have some work I need to do."

The various Egyptologists, archaeologists, experts, and assistants could be seen exchanging glances with one another. They didn't like it, but they had to obey. After all, hadn't the head of the expedition found yet another royal tomb where none was thought to be? Hadn't he uncovered more lost pharaohs than anyone else in the whole history of the world?

So what if he was a little strange? He was the best.

"Very well, Dr. Addams," the assistant said.

They filed out of the inner chamber of the great tomb, leaving Addams alone amid the treasures, dwarfed by the huge stone sarcophaguses. As the last person left, Addams said without turning his head, "And close the door behind you."

When the door was closed, Addams walked toward one of the great sarcophaguses. It was a struggle, but he managed to remove the lid at last.

He smiled and nodded when he saw the surface of the mummy case, as if it was just what he'd expected. He bent forward and rapped lightly on it with his knuckles.

"Knock knock," he said.

A voice creaky from long disuse spoke. "Er . . . who's there?"

Parker Addams, world-famous archaeologist, leaned close to the mummy case. "Morton sent me," he said.

Solve the puzzle, then create your own version of the creepy monster! First write the answers in the spaces below each clue. Then copy the numbered letters into the same numbered empty spaces on the following page. When all the blanks are filled in, you'll have the name of a famous monster. Then have fun drawing your own version of the Mystery Monster!

What am I?

1. I'm known for my way of getting around—on a broom!
Answer: I am a ___ ___ ___ ___ ___
(blank 4 = 1)

2. I'm a count from Transylvania, and "I vant to suck your blood!"
Answer: I am ___ ___ ___ ___ ___ ___ ___
(blank 4 = 3, blank 6 = 4)

3. I am a type of bat, and I, too, like sucking blood!
Answer: I am a ___ ___ ___ ___ ___ ___ ___
(blank 4 = 6)

4. When a house is haunted, I'm the one people blame.
Answer: I am a ___ ___ ___ ___ ___

5 (under the 3rd blank), 7 (under the 4th blank)

5. I'm found in a museum, wrapped tightly, in a tomb.
Answer: I am a ___ ___ ___ ___ ___

2 (under the 5th blank)

Mystery Monster:

___ ___ ___ ___ ___ ___ ___
1 2 3 4 5 6 7

Draw the Monster here:

About the Author

Tom B. Stone has written more than forty books for children. The author enjoys playing soccer, sailing, reading, hiking, biking, blading, and staying up late, but not anchovies, broccoli, squid, politicians, or scary movies. Stone lives in Sag Harbor, New York, with two dogs and three cats.